The Burning Bridge

The Burning Bridge
POUL ANDERSON

ÆGYPAN PRESS

This story was first published in the January, 1960, issue of *Astounding Science Fiction.*

Special thanks to Greg Weeks, Bruce Albrecht, Stephen Blundell, and the Online Distributed Proofreading Team (which can be found at http://www.pgdp.net).

The Burning Bridge
A publication of
ÆGYPAN PRESS

www.aegypan.com

*Usually there are two 'reasons' why
something is done; the reason why it
needs to be done, and, quite separate, the
reason people want to do it. The foul-up
starts when the reason-for-wanting
is satisfied . . . and the need remains!*

*T*he message was an electronic shout, the most powerful and tightly-beamed short-wave transmission which men could generate, directed with all the precision which mathematics and engineering could offer. Nevertheless that pencil must scrawl broadly over the sky, and for a long time, merely hoping to write on its target. For when distances are measured in light-weeks, the smallest errors grow monstrous.

As it happened, the attempt was successful. Communications Officer Anastas Mardikian had assembled his receiver after acceleration ceased — a big thing, surrounding the flagship *Ranger* like a spiderweb trapping a fly — and had kept it hopefully tuned over a wide band. The radio beam swept through, ghostly faint from dispersion, wave length doubled by Doppler effect, ragged with cosmic noise. An elaborate system of filters and amplifiers could make it no more than barely intelligible.

But that was enough.

Mardikian burst onto the bridge. He was young, and the months had not yet devoured the glory of his first deep-space voyage. "Sir!" he yelled. "A message . . . I just played back the recorder . . . from Earth!"

Fleet Captain Joshua Coffin started. That movement, in weightlessness, spun him off the deck. He stopped himself with a practiced hand, stiffened, and rapped back: "If you haven't yet learned regulations, a week of solitary confinement may give you a chance to study them."

"I . . . but, sir —" The other man retreated. His uniform made a loose rainbow splash across metal and plastic. Coffin alone, of all the fleet's company, held to the black garments of a space service long extinct.

"But, sir," said Mardikian. His voice seemed to have fallen off a high cliff. "Word from Earth!"

"Only the duty officer may enter the bridge without permission," Coffin reminded him. "If you had anything urgent to tell, there is an intercom."

"I thought —" choked Mardikian. He paused, then came to the free-fall equivalent of attention. Anger glittered in his eyes. "Sorry, sir."

Coffin hung quiet a while, looking at the dark young man in the brilliant clothes. *Forget it,* he said to himself. *Times are another. You went once to e Eridani, and almost ninety years had passed when you returned. Earth was like a foreign planet. This is as good as spacemen get to be nowadays, careless, superstitious, jabbering among each other in languages I don't understand. Thank God there are any recruits at all, and hope He will let there continue to be a few for what remains of your life.*

The duty officer, Hallmyer, was tall and blond and born in Lancashire; but he watched the other two with Asian eyes. No one spoke, though Mardikian breathed heavily. Stars filled the bow viewport, crowding a huge night.

Coffin sighed. "Very well," he said. "I'll let it pass this time."

After all, he reflected, a message from Earth was an event. Radio had, indeed, gone between Sol and Alpha Centauri, but that was with very special equipment. To pinpoint a handful of ships, moving at half the speed of light, and to do it so well that the comparatively small receiver Mardikian had erected would pick up the beam — Yes, the boy had some excuse for gladness.

"What was the signal?" Coffin inquired.

He expected it would only be routine, a test, so that engineers a lifetime hence could ask the returning fleet whether their transmission had registered. (If there were any engineers by then, on an Earth sinking into poverty and mysticism.)

Instead, Mardikian blurted: "Old Svoboda is dead. The new Psychologics Commissioner is Thomas . . . Thomson . . .

that part didn't record clearly . . . anyway, he must be sympathetic to the Constitutionalists. He's rescinded the educational decree — promised more consideration to provincial mores. Come hear for yourself, sir!"

Despite himself, Coffin whistled. "But that's why the e Eridani colony was being founded," he said. His words fell flat and silly into silence.

Hallmyer said, with the alien hiss in his English that Coffin hated, for it was like the Serpent in a once noble garden:

"Apparently the colony has no more reason to be started. But how shall we consult with three thousand would-be pioneers lying in deepsleep?"

"Shall we?" Coffin did not know why — not yet — but he felt his brain move with the speed of fear. "We've undertaken to deliver them to Rustum. In the absence of definite orders from Earth, are we even allowed to consider a change of plans . . . since a general vote can't be taken? Better avoid possible trouble and not even mention —" He broke off. Mardikian's face had become a mask of dismay.

"But, sir!" bleated the Com officer.

A chill rose up in Coffin. "You have already told," he said.

"Yes," whispered Mardikian. "I met Coenrad de Smet, he had come over to this ship for some repair parts, and . . . I never thought —"

"Exactly!" growled Coffin.

The fleet numbered fifteen, more than half the interstellar ships humankind possessed. But Earth's overlords had been as anxious to get rid of the Constitutionalists (the most stubborn ones, at least; the stay-at-homes were *ipso facto* less likely to be troublesome) as that science-minded, liberty-minded group of archaists were to escape being forcibly absorbed by modern society. Rustum, e Eridani II, was six parsecs away, forty-one years of travel, and barely habitable: but the only possible world yet discovered. A successful colony would be prestigious, and could do no harm; its failure would dispose of a thorn in the official ribs. Tying up fifteen ships for eight decades was all right too. Exploration was a dwindling activity, which interested fewer men each generation.

So Earth's government co-operated fully. It even provided speeches and music when the colonists embarked for the orbiting fleet. After which, Coffin thought, the government had doubtless grinned to itself and thanked its various heathen gods that that was over with.

"Only now," he muttered, "it isn't."

He free-sat in the *Ranger's* general room, a tall, bony, faintly grizzled Yankee, and waited. The austerity of the walls was broken by a few pictures. Coffin had wanted to leave them bare — since no one else would care for a view of the church where his father had preached, a hundred years ago, or be interested in a model of that catboat the boy Joshua had sailed on a bay which glittered in summers now forgotten — but even the theoretically absolute power of a fleet captain had its limits. At least the men nowadays were not making this room obscene with naked women. Though in all honesty, he wasn't sure he wouldn't rather have that than . . . brush-strokes on rice paper, the suggestion of a tree, and a classic ideogram. He did not understand the new generations.

The *Ranger* skipper, Nils Kivi, was like a breath of home: a small dapper Finn who had traveled with Coffin on the first e Eridani trip. They were not exactly friends, an admiral has no intimates, but they had been young in the same decade.

Actually, thought Coffin, *most of us spacemen are anachronisms. I could talk to Goldstein or Yamato or Pereira, to quite a few on this voyage, and not meet blank surprise when I mentioned a dead actor or hummed a dead song. But of course, they are all in unaging deepsleep now. We'll stand our one-year watches in turn, and be put back in the coldvats, and have no chance to talk till journey's end.*

"It may prove to be fun," mused Kivi.

"What?" asked Coffin.

"To walk around High America again, and fish in the Emperor River, and dig up our old camp," said Kivi. "We had some fine times on Rustum, along with all the work and danger."

Coffin was startled, that his own thoughts should have been so closely followed. "Yes," he agreed, remembering strange wild dawns on the Cleft edge, "that was a pretty good five years."

Kivi sighed. "Different this time," he said. "Now that I think about it, I am not sure I do want to go back. We had so much hope then — we were discoverers, walking where men had never even laid eyes before. Now the colonists will be the hopeful ones. We are just their transportation."

Coffin shrugged. "We must take what is given us, and be thankful."

"This time," said Kivi, "I will constantly worry: suppose I come home again and find my job abolished? No more space travel at all. If that happens, I refuse to be thankful."

Forgive him, Coffin asked his God. *It is cruel to watch the foundation of your life being gnawed away.*

Kivi's eyes lit up, the briefest flicker. "Of course," he said, "if we really do cancel this trip, and go straight back, we may not arrive too late. We may still find a few expeditions to new stars being organized, and get on their rosters."

Coffin tautened. Again he was unsure why he felt an emotion: now, anger. "I shall permit no disloyalty to the purpose for which we are engaged," he clipped.

"Oh, come off it," said Kivi. "Be rational. I don't know your reason for undertaking this wretched cruise. You had rank enough to turn down the assignment; no one else did. But you still want to explore as badly as I. If Earth didn't care about us, they would not have bothered to invite us back. Let us seize the opportunity while it lasts." He intercepted a reply by glancing at the wall chrono. "Time for our conference." He flicked the intership switch.

A panel came to life, dividing into fourteen sections, one for each accompanying vessel. One or two faces peered from each. The craft which bore only supplies and sleeping crewmen were represented by their captains. Those which had colonists also revealed a civilian spokesman.

Coffin studied every small image in turn. The spacemen he knew, they all belonged to the Society and even those born long after him had much in common. There was a necessary minimum discipline of mind and body, and the underlying dream for which all else had been traded: new horizons under new suns. Not that spacemen indulged in such poetics; they had too much work to do.

The colonists were something else. Coffin shared things with them — predominantly North American background, scientific habit of thought, distrust of all governments. But few Constitutionalists had any religion; those who did were Romish, Jewish, Buddhist, or otherwise alien to him. All were tainted with the self-indulgence of this era: they had written into their covenant that only physical necessity could justify moralizing legislation, and that free speech was limited only by personal libel. Coffin thought sometimes he would be glad to see the last of them.

"Are you all prepared?" he began. "Very well, let's get down to business. It's unfortunate the Com officer gossiped so loosely. He stirred up a hornet's nest." Coffin saw that few understood the idiom. "He made discontent which threatens this whole project, and which we must now deal with."

Coenrad de Smet, colonist aboard the *Scout,* smiled in an irritating way he had. "You would simply have concealed the fact?" he asked.

"It would have made matters easier," said Coffin stiffly.

"In other words," said de Smet, "you know better what we might want than we do ourselves. That, sir, is the kind of arrogance we hoped to escape. No man has the right to suppress any information bearing on public affairs."

A low voice, with a touch of laughter, said through a hood: "And you accuse Captain Coffin of preaching!"

The New Englander's eyes were drawn to her. Not that he could see through the shapeless gown and mask, such as hid all the waking women; but he had met Teresa Zeleny on Earth. Hearing her now was somehow like remembering Indian summer on a wooded hilltop, a century ago.

An involuntary smile quirked his lips. "Thank you," he said. "Do you, Mr. de Smet, know what the sleeping colonists might want? Have you any right to decide for *them?* And yet we can't wake them, even the adults, to vote. There simply isn't room; if nothing else, the air regenerators couldn't supply that much oxygen. That's why I felt it best to tell no one, until we were actually at Rustum. Then those who wished could return with the fleet, I suppose."

"We could rouse them a few at a time, let them vote, and put them back to sleep," suggested Teresa Zeleny.

"It would take weeks," said Coffin. "You, of all people, should know metabolism isn't lightly stopped, or easily restored."

"If you could see my face," she said, again with a chuckle, "I would grimace amen. I'm so sick of tending inert human flesh that . . . well, I'm glad they're only women and girls, because if I also had to massage and inject men I'd take a vow of chastity!"

Coffin blushed, cursed himself for blushing, and hoped she couldn't see it over the telecircuit. He noticed Kivi grin.

*K*ivi provided the merciful interruption. "Your few-at-a-time proposal is pointless anyhow," he said. "In the course of those weeks, we would pass the critical date."

"What's that?" asked a young girl's voice.

"You don't know?" said Coffin, surprised.

"Let it pass for now," broke in Teresa. Once again, as several times before, Coffin admired her decisiveness. She cut through nonsense with a man's speed and a woman's practicality. "Take our word for it, June, if we don't turn about within two months, we'll do better to go on to Rustum. So, voting is out. We could wake a few sleepers, but those already conscious are really as adequate a statistical sample."

Coffin nodded. She spoke for five women on her ship, who stood a year-watch caring for two hundred ninety-five asleep. The one hundred twenty who would not be restimulated for such duty during the voyage, were children. The proportion on the other nine colonist-laden vessels was similar; the crew totaled one thousand six hundred twenty, with forty-five up and about at all times. Whether the die was cast by less than two percent, or by four or five percent, was hardly significant.

"Let's recollect exactly what the message was," said Coffin. "The educational decree which directly threatened your Constitutionalist way of life has been withdrawn. You're no worse off now than formerly — and no better, though there's a hint of further concessions in the future. You're invited home again. That's all. We have not picked up any other transmissions. It seems very little data on which to base so large a decision."

"It's an even bigger one, to continue," said de Smet. He leaned forward, a bulky man, until he filled his little screen. Hardness rang in his tones. "We were able people, economically rather well off. I daresay Earth already misses our services, especially in technological fields. Your own report makes Rustum out a grim place; many of us would die there. Why should we not turn home?"

"Home," whispered someone.

The word filled a sudden quietness, like water filling a cup, until quietness brimmed over with it. Coffin sat listening to the voice of his ship, generators, ventilators, regulators, and he began to hear a beat frequency which was *Home, home, home.*

Only his home was gone. His father's church was torn down for an Oriental temple, and the woods where October had burned were cleared for another tentacle of city, and the bay was enclosed to make a plankton farm. For him, only a spaceship remained, and the somehow cold hope of heaven.

A very young man said, almost to himself: "I left a girl back there."

"I had a little sub," said another. "I used to poke around the Great Barrier Reef, skindiving out the air lock or loafing on the surface. You wouldn't believe how blue the waves could be. They tell me on Rustum you can't come down off the mountain tops."

"But we'd have the whole planet to ourselves," said Teresa Zeleny.

One with a gentle scholar's face answered: "That may be precisely the trouble, my dear. Three thousand of us, counting children, totally isolated from the human mainstream. Can we hope to build a civilization? Or even maintain one?"

"Your problem, pop," said the officer beside him dryly, "is that there are no medieval manuscripts on Rustum."

"I admit it," said the scholar. "I thought it more important my children grow up able to use their minds. But if it turns out they can do so on Earth — How much chance will the first generations on Rustum have to sit down and really think, anyway?"

"Would there even be a next generation on Rustum?"

"One and a quarter gravities — I can feel it now."

"Synthetics, year after year of synthetics and hydroponics, till we can establish an ecology. I had steak on Earth, once in a while."

"My mother couldn't come. Too frail. But she's paid for a hundred years of deepsleep, all she could afford . . . just in case I do return."

"I designed skyhouses. They won't build anything on Rustum much better than sod huts, in my lifetime."

"Do you remember moonlight on the Grand Canyon?"

"Do you remember Beethoven's Ninth in the Federal Concert Hall?"

"Do you remember that funny little Midlevel bar, where we all drank beer and sang *Lieder?*"

"Do you remember?"

"Do you remember?"

*T*eresa Zeleny shouted across their voices: "In Anker's name! What are you thinking about? If you care so little, you should never have embarked in the first place!"

It brought back the silence, not all at once but piece by piece, until Coffin could pound the table and call for order. He looked straight at her hidden eyes and said: "Thank you, Miss Zeleny. I was expecting tears to be uncorked any moment."

One of the girls snuffled behind her mask.

Charles Lochaber, speaking for the *Courier* colonists, nodded. "Aye, 'tis a blow to our purpose. I am not so sairtain I myself would vote to continue, did I feel the message was to be trusted."

"What?" De Smet's square head jerked up from between his shoulders.

Lochaber grinned without much humor. "The government has been getting more arbitrary each year," he said. "They were ready enough to let us go, aye. But they may regret it now — not because we could ever be any active threat, but because we will be a subversive example, up there in Earth's sky. Or just because we will *be.* Mind ye, I know not for sairtain; but 'tis possible they decided we are safer dead, and this is to trick us back. 'Twould be characteristic dictatorship behavior."

"Of all the fantastic —" gasped an indignant female voice.

Teresa broke in: "Not as wild as you might think, dear. I have read a little history, and I don't mean that censored pap which passes for it nowadays. But there's another possibility, which I think is just as alarming. That message may be perfectly honest and sincere. But will it still be true when we get back? Remember how long that will take! And even if we could return overnight, to an Earth which welcomed us home, what guarantee would there be that our children, or our grandchildren, won't suffer the same troubles as us, without the same chance to break free?"

"Ye vote, then, to carry on?" asked Lochaber.

Pride answered: "Of course."

"Good lass. I, too."

Kivi raised his hand. Coffin recognized him, and the spaceman said: "I am not sure the crew ought not to have a voice in this also."

"What?" De Smet grew red. He gobbled for a moment before he could get out: "Do you seriously think you could elect us to settle on that annex of hell — and then come home to Earth yourselves?"

"As a matter of fact," said Kivi, smiling, "I suspect the crew would prefer to return at once. I know I would. Seven years may make a crucial difference."

"If a colony is planted, though," said Coffin, "it might provide the very inspiration which space travel needs to survive."

"Hm-m-m. Perhaps. I shall have to think about that."

"I hope you realize," said the very young man with ornate sarcasm, "that every second we sit here arguing takes us one hundred fifty thousand kilometers farther from home."

"Dinna fash yourself," said Lochaber. "Whatever we do, that girl of yours will be an auld carline before you reach Earth."

De Smet was still choking at Kivi: "You lousy little ferryman, if you think you can make pawns of us —"

And Kivi stretched his lips in anger and growled, "If you do not watch your language, you clodhugger, I will come over there and stuff you down your own throat."

"Order!" yelled Coffin. "Order!"

Teresa echoed him: "Please . . . for all our lives' sake . . . don't you know where we are? You've got a few centimeters of wall between you and zero! Please, whatever we do, we can't fight or we'll never see any planet again!"

But she did not say it weeping, or as a beggary. It was almost a mother's voice — strange, in an unmarried woman — and it quieted the male snarling more than Coffin's shouts.

The fleet captain said finally: "That will do. You're all too worked up to think. Debate is adjourned sixteen hours. Discuss the problem with your shipmates, get some sleep, and report the consensus at the next meeting."

"Sixteen hours?" yelped someone. "Do you know how much return time that adds?"

"You heard me," said Coffin. "Anybody who wants to argue may do so from the brig. Dismissed!"

He snapped off the switch.

Kivi, temper eased, gave him a slow confidential grin. "That heavy-father act works nearly every time, no?"

Coffin pushed from the table. "I'm going out," he said. His voice sounded harsh to him, a stranger's. "Carry on."

He had never felt so alone before, not even the night his father died. *O God, who spake unto Moses in the wilderness, reveal now thy will.* But God was silent, and Coffin turned blindly to the only other help he could think of.

*S*pace armored, he paused a moment in the air lock before continuing. He had been an astronaut for twenty-five years — for a century if you added time in the vats — but he could still not look upon naked creation without fear.

An infinite blackness flashed: stars beyond stars, to the bright ghost-road of the Milky Way and on out to other galaxies and flocks of galaxies, until the light which a telescope might now register had been born before the Earth. Looking from his air-lock cave, past the radio web and the other ships, Coffin felt himself drown in enormousness, coldness, and total silence — though he knew that this vacuum burned and roared with man-destroying energies, roiled like currents of gas and dust more massive than planets and travailed with the birth of new suns — and he said to himself the most dreadful of names, *I am that I am,* and sweat formed chilly little globules under his arms.

This much a man could see within the Solar System. Traveling at half light-speed stretched the human mind still further, till often it ripped across and another lunatic was shoved into deepsleep. For aberration redrew the sky, crowding stars toward the bows, so that the ships plunged toward a cloud of Doppler hell-blue. The constellations lay thinly abeam, you looked out upon the dark. Aft, Sol was still the brightest object in heaven, but it had gained a sullen red tinge, as if already grown old, as if the prodigal would return from far places to find his home buried under ice.

What is man that thou art mindful of him? The line gave its accustomed comfort; for, after all, the Sun-maker had also wrought this flesh, atom by atom, and at the very least would think it worthy of hell. Coffin had never understood how his atheist colleagues endured free space.

Well —

He took aim at the next hull and fired his little spring-powered crossbow. A light line unreeled behind the magnetic bolt. He tested its security with habitual care, pulled himself along until he reached the companion ship, yanked the bolt loose and fired again, and so on from hull to slowly orbiting hull, until he reached the *Pioneer.*

Its awkward ugly shape was like a protective wall against the stars. Coffin drew himself past the ion tubes, now cold. Their skeletal structure seemed impossibly frail to have hurled forth peeled atoms at one half c. Mass tanks bulked around the vessel; allowing for deceleration, plus a small margin, the mass ratio was about nine to one. Months would be required at Rustum to refine enough reaction material for the home voyage. Meanwhile such of the crew as were not thus engaged would help the colony get established —

If it ever did!

Coffin reached the forward air lock and pressed the "doorbell." The outer valve opened for him, and he cycled through. First Officer Karamchand met him and helped him doff armor. The other man on duty found an excuse to approach and listen; for monotony was as corrosive out here as distance and strangeness.

"Ah, sir. What brings you over?"

Coffin braced himself. Embarrassment roughened his tone: "I want to see Miss Zeleny."

"Of course — But why come yourself? I mean, the telecircuit —"

"In person!" barked Coffin.

"What?" escaped the crewman. He propelled himself backward in terror of a wigging. Coffin ignored it.

"Emergency," he snapped. "Please intercom her and arrange for a private discussion."

"Why . . . why . . . yes, sir. At once. Will you wait here . . . I mean . . . yes, sir!" Karamchand shot down the corridor.

Coffin felt a sour smile on his own lips. He could understand if they got confused. His own law about the women had been like steel, and now he violated it himself.

The trouble was, he thought, no one knew if it was even required. Until now there had been few enough women crossing space, and then only within the Solar System, on segregated ships. There was no background of interstellar experience. It seemed reasonable, though, that a man on his year-watch should not be asked to tend deepsleeping female colonists. (Or vice versa!) The idea revolted Coffin personally; but for once the psychotechs had agreed with him. And, of course, waking men and women, freely intermingling, were potentially even more explosive. Haremlike seclusion appeared the only answer; and husband and wife were not to be awake at the same time.

Bad enough to see women veiled when there was a telecircuit conference. (Or did the masks make matters still worse, by challenging the imagination? Who knew?) Best seal off the living quarters and coldvat sections of the craft which bore them. Crewmen standing watches on those particular ships had better return to their own vessels to sleep and eat.

Coffin braced his muscles. *The rules wouldn't apply if a large meteor struck,* he reminded himself. *What has come up is more dangerous than that. So never mind what anyone thinks.*

Karamchand returned to salute him and say breathlessly: "Miss Zeleny will see you, captain. This way, if you please."

"Thanks." Coffin followed to the main bulkhead. The women had its doorkey. Now the door stood ajar. Coffin pushed himself through so hard that he overshot and caromed off the farther wall.

Teresa laughed. She closed the door and locked it. "Just to make them feel safe out there," she said. "Poor well-meaning men! Welcome, captain."

*H*e turned about, almost dreading the instant. Her tall form was decent in baggy coveralls, but she had dropped the mask. She was not pretty, he supposed: broad-faced, square-jawed, verging on spinsterhood. But he had liked her way of smiling.

"I —" He found no words.

"Follow me." She led him down a short passage, hand-over-hand along the null-gee rungs. "I've warned the other girls to stay away. You needn't fear being shocked." At the end of the hall was a little partitioned-off room. Few enough personal goods could be taken along, but she had made this place hers, a painting, a battered Shakespeare, the works of Anker, a microplayer. Her tapes ran to Bach, late Beethoven and Strauss, music which could be studied endlessly. She took hold of a stanchion and nodded, all at once grown serious.

"What do you want to ask me, captain?"

Coffin secured himself by the crook of an arm and stared at his hands. The fingers strained against each other. "I wish I could give you a clear reply," he said, very low and with difficulty. "You see, I've never met anything like this before. If it involved only men, I guess I could handle the problem. But there are women along, and children."

"And you want a female viewpoint. You're wiser than I had realized. But why me?"

He forced himself to meet her eyes. "You appear the most sensible of the women awake."

"Really!" She laughed. "I appreciate the compliment, but must you deliver it in that parade-ground voice, and glare at me to boot? Relax, captain." She cocked her head, studying him. Then: "Several of the girls don't get this business of the critical point. I tried to explain, but I was only an R.N. at home, and I'm afraid I muddled it rather. Could you put it in words of one and a half syllables?"

"Do you mean the equal-time point?"

"The Point of No Return, some of them call it."

"Nonsense! It's only — Well, look at it this way. We accelerated from Sol at one gravity. We dare not apply more acceleration, even though we could, because so many articles aboard have been lightly built to save mass — the coldvats, for example. They'd collapse under their own weight, and the persons within would die, if we went as much as one-point-five gee. Very well. It took us about one hundred eighty days to reach maximum velocity. In the course of that period, we covered not quite one-and-a-half light-months. We will now go free for almost forty years. At the end of that time, we'll decelerate at one gee for some one hundred eighty days, covering an additional light-month and a half, and enter the e Eridani System with low relative speed. Our star-to-star orbit was plotted with care, but of course the errors add up to many Astronomical Units; furthermore, we have to maneuver, put our ships in orbit about Rustum, send ferry craft back and forth. So we carry a reaction-mass reserve which allows us a total velocity change of about one thousand kilometers per second after journey's end.

"Now imagine we had changed our minds immediately after reaching full speed. We'd still have to decelerate in order to return. So we'd be almost a quarter light-year from Sol, a year after departure, before achieving relative rest. Then, to come back three light-months at one thousand K.P.S. takes roughly seventy-two years. But the whole round trip as originally scheduled, with a one-year layover at Rustum, runs just about eighty-three years!

"Obviously there's some point in time beyond which we can actually get home quicker by staying with the original plan. This date lies after eight months of free fall, or not quite fourteen months from departure. We're only a couple of months from the critical moment right now; if we start back at once, we'll still have been gone from Earth for about seventy-six years. Each day we wait adds months to the return trip. No wonder there's impatience!"

"And the relativity clock paradox makes it worse," Teresa said.

"Well, not too much," Coffin decided. "The tau factor is 0.87. Shipboard time during eighty years of free fall amounts to about seventy years; so far the difference isn't significant. And anyhow, we'll all spend most of the time in deepsleep. What they're afraid of, the ones who want to go back, is that the Earth they knew will have slipped away from them."

She nodded. "Can't they understand it already has?" she said.

It was like a blade stabbed into Coffin. Though he could not see why that should be: surely he, of all men, knew how relentlessly time flowed. He had already come back once, to an Earth scarcely recognizable. The Society had been a kind of fixed point, but even it had changed; and he — like Kivi, like all of them — was now haunted by the fear of returning again and not finding any other spacemen whatsoever.

But when she spoke it —

"Maybe they're afraid to understand," he said.

"You keep surprising me, captain," said Teresa with a hint of her smile. "You actually show a bit of human sympathy."

And, thought a far-off part of Coffin, *you showed enough to put me at ease by getting me to lecture you with safe impersonal figures.* But he didn't mind. The fact was that now he could free-sit, face to face, alone, and talk to her like a friend.

"Since we could only save about seven years by giving up at once," he said, "I admit I'm puzzled why so many people are so anxious about it. Couldn't we go on as planned and decide things at Rustum?"

"I think not," said Teresa. "You see, nobody in his right mind wants to be a pioneer. To explore, yes; to settle rich new country with known and limited hazards, yes; but not to risk his children, his whole racial future, on a wild gamble. This group was driven into space by a conflict which just couldn't be settled at home. If that conflict has ended —"

"But . . . you and Lochaber . . . you pointed out that it had *not* ended. That at best this is a breathing spell."

"Still, they'd like to believe otherwise, wouldn't they? I mean, at least believe they have a fighting chance on Earth."

"All right," said Coffin. "But it looks a safe bet, that there are a number of deepsleepers who'd agree with you, who'd think their chances are actually better on Rustum. Why can't we take them there first? It seems only fair."

"Uh-uh." Her hair was short, but it floated in loose waves when she shook her head, and light rippled mahogany across it. "You've been there and I haven't, but I've studied your reports. A handful couldn't survive. Three thousand is none too many. It will have to be unanimous, whatever is decided."

"I was trying to avoid that conclusion," he said wearily, "but if you agree — Well, can't we settle the argument at Rustum, after they've looked the place over?"

"No. And I'll tell you why, captain," she said. "I know Coenrad de Smet well, and one or two others. Good men . . . don't get me wrong . . . but born politicians, intuitive rather than logical thinkers. They believe, quite honestly, it's best to go back. And, of course, the timid and lazy and selfish ones will support them. They don't want to risk having Rustum there, a whole new world for the taking — and the vote to go against them. I've seen plenty of your photographs, captain. They were so beautiful, some of them, that I can hardly wait for the reality. I know — and so does de Smet — High America is a magnificent place. Room, freedom, unpoisoned air. We'll remember all that we hated on Earth and that isn't on Rustum; we'll reflect much more soberly how long a time will have passed before we could possibly get back, and what a gamble we'd be taking on finding a tolerable situation there. The extra quarter gee won't seem so bad till it's time for heavy manual labor; the alien biochemistry won't bother us much till we have to stop eating rations and start trying to farm; the isolation won't really be felt till your spaceships have departed and we're all the humanity there is for more than twenty light-years.

"No . . . de Smet won't risk it. He might get caught up in the glamour himself!"

Coffin murmured thoughtfully: "After only a few days of deceleration, there won't be enough reaction mass to do anything but continue home."

"De Smet knows that, too," said Teresa. "Captain, you can make a hard decision and stick to it. That's why you have your job. But maybe you forget how few people can — how most of us pray someone will come along and tell us what to do. Even under severe pressure, the decision to go to Rustum was difficult. Now that there's a chance to undo it, go back to being safe and comfortable — but still a real risk that by the time we get home, Earth will no longer be safe *or* comfortable — we've been forced to decide all over again. It's agony, captain! De Smet is a strong man, in his way. He'll compel us to do the irrevocable, as soon as possible, just because it will make a final commitment. Once we've turned far enough back, it'll be out of our hands and we can stop thinking."

He regarded her with a sort of wonder. "But you look calm enough," he said.

"I made my decision back on Earth," she answered. "I've seen no reason to change it."

"What do the women think?" he asked, leaping back to safely denumerable things.

"Most want to give up, of course." She said it with a mildness which softened the judgment. "Few of them really wanted to come in the first place. They did so only because their men insisted. Women are much too practical to care about a philosophy, or a frontier, or anything except their families."

"Do you?" he challenged her.

She shrugged ruefully. "I've no family, captain. At the same time, I suppose . . . a sense of humor? . . . kept me from sublimating it into a Cause of any kind." Counterattacking: "Why do you care what we do, captain?"

"Why?" He was taken aback, and found himself stammering. "Why . . . because . . . I'm in charge —"

"Oh, yes. But isn't it more than that? You spent years on Earth lecturing about Rustum and its colonization. I think it must be a deep symbol to you. Don't worry, I won't go analytic. I happen to think, myself, that this colony is enormously important, objectively speaking, I mean. If our race muffs this chance, we may never get another. But you and I wouldn't care about that, not really, unless it was personally important too. Would we? Why did you accept this thankless job, commanding a colonial fleet? It can't be an itch to explore. Rustum's already been visited once, and you'll have precious little time to carry on any further studies. You could have been off to some star where men have never traveled at all. Do you see, captain? You're not a bit more cold-blooded about this than I. You *want* that colony planted."

She stopped, laughed, and color went across her face. "Oh, dear, I do chatter, don't I? Pardon me. Let's get back to business."

"I think," said Coffin, slowly and jaggedly, "I'm beginning to realize what's involved."

She settled back and listened.

He bent a leg around a stanchion to hold his lean black frame in place and beat one fist softly into the palm of another. "Yes, it is an emotional issue," he said, the words carving the thoughts to shape. "Logic has nothing to do with it. There are some who want so badly to go to Rustum and be free, or whatever they hope to be there, that they'll dice with their lives for the privilege — and their wives' and children's lives. Others went reluctantly, against their own survival instincts, and now that they think they see a way of retreat, something they can justify to themselves, they'll fight any man who tries to bar it. Yes. It's a ghastly situation.

"One way or another, the decision has got to be made soon. And the facts can't be hidden. Every deepsleeper must be wakened and nursed to health by someone now conscious. The word will pass, year after year, always to a different combination of spacemen and colonists, with always a proportion who're furious about what was decided while they slept. No, furious is too weak a word. Onward or backward, whichever way we go, we've struck at the emotional roots of people. And interstellar space can break the calmest men. How long before just the wrong percentage of malcontents, weaklings, and shaky sanities goes on duty? What's going to happen then?"

He sucked in an uneven breath. "I'm sorry," he faltered. "I should not —"

"Blow off steam? Why not?" she asked calmly. "Would it be better to keep on being the iron man, till one day you put a pistol to your head?"

"You see," he said in his misery, "I'm *responsible.* Men and women . . . all the little children — But I'll be in deepsleep. I'd go crazy if I tried to stay awake the whole voyage; the organism can't take it. I'll be asleep, and there'll be nothing I can do, but these ships were given into my care!"

He began to shiver. She took both his hands. Neither of them spoke for a long while.

*W*hen he left the *Pioneer,* Coffin felt oddly hollow, as if he had opened his chest and pulled out heart and lungs. But his mind functioned with machine precision. For that he was grateful to Teresa: she had helped him discover what the facts were. It was a brutal knowledge, but without such understanding the expedition might well be doomed.

Or might it? Dispassionately, now, Coffin estimated chances. Either they went on to Rustum or they turned back;

in either case, the present likelihood of survival was — fifty-fifty? Well, you couldn't gauge it in percentages. Doubtless more safety lay in turning back. But even there the odds were such that no sane man would willingly gamble. Certainly the skipper had no right to take the hazard, if he could avoid it by any means.

But what means were there?

As he hauled himself toward the *Ranger*, Coffin watched the receiver web grow in his eyes, till it snared a distorted Milky Way. It seemed very frail to have carried so much hell. And, indeed, it would have to be dismantled before deceleration. No trick to sabotage the thing. *If only I had known!*

Or if someone on Earth, the villain or well-meaning fool or whatever he was who wrote that first message . . . if only he would send another. "Ignore preceding. Educational decree still in force." Or something. But no. Such things didn't happen. A man had to make his own luck, in an angry world.

Coffin sighed and clamped boot-soles to his flagship's air lock.

Mardikian helped him through. When he removed his hoarfrosted space helmet, Coffin saw how the boy's mouth quivered. A few hours had put years on Mardikian.

He was in medical whites. Unnecessarily, to break the silence with any inane remark, Coffin said: "Going on vat duty, I see."

"Yes, sir." A mutter. "My turn." The armor made a lot of noise while they stowed it. "We'll need some more ethanol soon, captain," blurted Mardikian desperately.

"What for?" grumbled Coffin. He had often wished the stuff were not indispensable. He alone had the key to its barrel. Some masters allowed a small liquor ration on voyage, and said Coffin was only disguising prejudice in claiming it added risk. ("What the devil *can* happen in interstellar orbit? The only reason anyone stays conscious at all is the machinery to care properly for sleepers would mass more than the extra supplies do. You can issue the grog when a man comes off watch, can't you? Oh, never mind, never mind! I'm just grateful I don't ship under you!")

"Gammagen fixative . . . and so on . . . sir," stumbled Mardikian. "Mr. Hallmyer will . . . make the requisition as usual."

"All right." Coffin faced his radio man, captured the fearful eyes and would not let them go. "Have there been any further communications?" he snapped.

"From Earth? No. No, sir. I . . . I wouldn't really expect it . . . we're about at the . . . the . . . the limit of reception now. It's almost a miracle, sir, I suppose, that we picked up the first. Of course, we might get another —" Mardikian's voice trailed off.

Coffin continued to stare. At last: "They've been giving you a hard time, haven't they?"

"What?"

"The ones like Lochaber, who want to go on. They wish you'd had the sense to keep your mouth shut, at least till you consulted me. And then others, like de Smet, have said the opposite. Even over telecircuit, it's no fun being a storm center, is it?"

"No, sir —"

*C*offin turned away. Why torment the fellow more? This thing had happened, that was all. And the fewer who realized the danger, and were thereby put under still greater strain, the less that danger would be.

"Avoid such disputes," said Coffin. "Most especially, don't brood over those which do arise. That's just begging for a nervous breakdown — out here. Carry on."

Mardikian gulped and went aft.

Coffin drifted athwartships. The vessel thrummed around him.

He was not on watch, and had no desire to share the bridge with whoever was. He should eat something, but the idea was nauseating; he should try to sleep, but that would be useless. How long had he been with Teresa, while she cleared his mind and gave him what comfort she had to offer? A couple of hours. In fourteen hours or less, he must confront the spokesmen of crew and colonists. And meanwhile the fleet seethed.

On Earth, he thought wearily, a choice between going on and turning back would not have drawn men so close to insanity, even if the time elements had been the same. But Earth was long domesticated. Maybe, centuries ago, when a few wind-powered hulks wallowed forth upon hugeness, unsure whether they might sail off the world's edge — maybe then there had been comparable dilemmas. Yes . . . hadn't Columbus' men come near mutiny? Even unknown, though, and monster-peopled by superstition, Earth had not been as cruel an environment as space; nor had a caravel been as unnatural as a spaceship. Minds could never have disintegrated as quickly in mid-ocean as between the stars.

Coffin grew aware, startled, that he had wandered to the radio shack.

He entered. It was a mere cubbyhole, one wall occupied by gleaming electronic controls, the rest full of racked equipment, tools, testers, spare parts, half-assembled units for this and that special purpose. The fleet did not absolutely need a Com officer — any spaceman could do the minimal jobs, and any officer had intensive electronics training — but Mardikian was a good, conscientious, useful technician.

His trouble was, perhaps, only that he was human.

Coffin pulled himself to the main receiver. A tape whirred slowly between spools, preserving what the web gathered. Coffin looked at a clipboard. Mardikian had written half an hour ago: "Nothing received. Tape wiped and reset, 1530 hr." Maybe since then — ? Coffin flipped a switch. A scanner went quickly through the recording, found only cosmic noise — none of the orderliness which would have meant code or speech — and informed the man.

Now if it had just —

Coffin grew rigid. He floated among the mechanisms for a long time, blank-eyed as they, and alone the quick harsh breath showed him to be alive.

O God, help me do that which is right.

But what is right?

I should wrestle with Thy angel until I knew. But there is no time. Lord, be not wroth with me because I have no time.

Anguish ebbed. Coffin got busy.

Decision would be reached at the meeting, fourteen hours hence. A message which was to make a substantial difference ought to be received before then. But not very much before; nor too late, eleventh-hour-reprieve style, either.

But first, what should its wording be? Coffin didn't have to look up the last one. It was branded on his brain. An invitation to return and talk matters over. But necessarily short, compact, with minimum redundancy: which meant an increased danger of misinterpretation.

He braced himself before the typer and began to compose, struck out his first words and started again, and again and again. It had to be exactly right. A mere cancellation of the previous message wouldn't do after all. Too pat. And a suspicion, brooded on during a year-watch, could be as deadly as an outright sense of betrayal. So. . . .

Since fleet now approaching equal-time point, quick action necessary. Colonization plans abandoned. Expedition ordered, repeat ordered to return to Earth. Education decree already rescinded (a man back home wouldn't be certain the first beam had made contact) *and appeals for further concessions will be permitted through proper channels. Constitutionalists reminded that their first duty is to put their skills at disposal of society.*

Would that serve? Coffin read it over. It didn't contradict the first one; it only changed a suggestion to a command, as if someone were growing more frantic by the hour. (And a picture of near-chaos in government wasn't attractive, was it?) The bit about "proper channels" underlined that speech was not free on Earth, and that the bureaucracy could restore the school decree anytime it wished. The pompous last sentence ought to irritate men who had turned their backs on the thing which Terrestrial society was becoming.

Maybe it could be improved, though — Coffin resumed work.

When he ripped out his last version, he was astonished to note that two hours had passed. Already? The ship seemed very quiet. Too quiet. He grew feverishly aware that anyone might break in on him at any time.

The tape could run for a day, but was usually checked and wiped every six or eight hours. Coffin decided to put his words on it at a spot corresponding to seven hours hence. Mardikian would have come off vat duty, but probably be asleep; he wouldn't play back until shortly before the council meeting.

Coffin turned to a small auxiliary recorder. He had to tape his voice through a circuit which would alter it beyond recognition. And, of course, the whole thing had to be blurred, had to fade and come back, had to be full of squeals and buzzes and the crackling talk of the stars. No easy job to blend all those elements, in null-gee at that. Coffin lost himself in the task. He dared not do otherwise, for then he would be alone with himself.

Plug in this modulator, add an oscillation — Let's see, where's that slide rule, what quantities do you want for —

"What are you doing?"

Coffin twisted about. Fingers clamped on his heart.

Mardikian floated in the doorway, looking dazed and afraid as he saw who the intruder was. "What's wrong, sir?" he asked.

"You're on watch," breathed Coffin.

"Tea break, sir, and I thought I'd check and —" The boy pushed himself into the shack. Coffin saw him framed in meters and transformer banks, like some futuristic saint. But sweat glistened on the dark young face, broke free and drifted in tiny spheroids toward the ventilator.

"Get out of here," said Coffin thickly. And then: "No! I don't mean that! Stay where you are!"

"But —" Almost, the captain could read a mind: *If the old man has gone space-dizzy, name of fate, what's to become of us all?* "Yes, sir."

Coffin licked sandy lips. "It's okay," he said. "You surprised me, our nerves are on edge. That's why I hollered."

"S-s-sorry, sir."

"Anyone else around?"

"No, sir. All on duty or —" *I shouldn't have told him that!* Coffin read. *Now he knows I'm alone with him!*

"It's okay, son," repeated the captain. But his voice came out like a buzz saw cutting through bone. "I had a little project here I was, uh, playing with, and . . . uh —"

"Yes, sir. Of course." *Humor him till I can get away. Then see Mr. Kivi. Let him take the responsibility. I don't want it! I don't want to be the skipper, with nobody between me and the sky. It's too much. It'll crack a man wide open.*

Mardikian's trapped eyes circled the little room. They fell on the typer, and the drafts which Coffin had not yet destroyed.

Silence closed in.

"Well," said Coffin at last. "Now you know."

"Yes, sir." Mardikian could scarcely be heard.

"I'm going to fake this onto the receiver tape."

"B-b . . . Yes, sir." *Humor him!* Mardikian was drawn bowstring tight, his nostrils flared by terror.

"You see," rasped Coffin, "it has to look genuine. This ought to get their backs up. They'll be more united on colonizing Rustum than they ever were before. At the same time, I can resist them, claim I have my orders to turn about and don't want to get into trouble. Finally, of course, I'll let myself be talked into continuing, however reluctantly. So no one will suspect me of . . . fraud."

Mardikian's lips moved soundlessly. He was close to hysteria, Coffin saw.

"It's unavoidable," the captain said, and cursed himself for the roughness in his tone. Though maybe no orator could persuade this boy. What did he know of psychic breaking stress, who had never been tried to his own limit? "We'll have to keep the secret, you and I, or —" No, what was the use? Within Mardikian's small experience, it was so much more natural to believe that one man, Coffin, had gone awry, than to understand a month-by-month rotting of the human soul under loneliness and frustration.

"Yes, sir," Mardikian husked. "Of course, sir."

Even if he meant that, Coffin thought, *he might talk in his sleep. Or I might; but the admiral, alone of all the fleet, has a completely private room.*

He racked his tools, most carefully, and faced about. Mardikian shoved away, bulging-eyed. "No," whispered Mardikian. "No. Please."

He opened his mouth to scream, but he didn't get time. Coffin chopped him on the neck. As he doubled up, Coffin gripped him with legs and one hand, balled the other fist, and hit him often in the solar plexus.

Mardikian rolled in the air like a drowned man.

Swiftly, then, Coffin towed him down the corridor, to the pharmacy room. He unlocked the alcohol barrel, tapped a hypo, diluted it with enough water, and injected. Lucky the fleet didn't carry a real psychiatrist; if you broke, you went into deepsleep and weren't revived till you got home again to the clinics.

Coffin dragged the boy to a point near the air lock. Then he shouted. Hallmyer came from the bridge. "He started raving and attacked me," panted the captain. "I had to knock him out."

Mardikian was revived for a check-up, but since he only mumbled incoherently, he was given a sedative. Two men began processing him for the vat. Coffin said he would make sure that the Com officer hadn't damaged any equipment. He went back to the shack.

*T*eresa Zeleny met him. She did not speak, but led him to her room again.

"Well," he said, strangling on it, "so we're continuing to Rustum, by unanimous vote. Aren't you happy?"

"I was," she said quietly, "till now, when I see that you aren't. I hardly think you're worried about legal trouble on Earth; you have authority to ignore orders if the situation warrants. So what is the matter?"

He stared beyond her. "I shouldn't have come here at all," he said. "But I had to talk with someone, and only you might understand. Will you bear with me a few minutes? I won't bother you again."

"Not till Rustum." Her smile was a gesture of compassion. "And it's no bother." After waiting a bit: "What did you want to say?"

He told her, in short savage words.

She grew a little pale. "The kid was actually dead drunk, and they didn't know it when they processed him?" she said. "That's a grave risk. He might not live."

"I know," said Coffin, and covered his eyes.

Her hand fell on his shoulder. "I suppose you've done the only possible thing," she said with much gentleness. "Or, if there was a better way, you didn't have time to think of it."

He said through his fingers, while his head turned away from her: "If you don't tell on me, and I know you won't, then you're violating your own principles, too: total information, free discussion and decision. Aren't you?"

She sighed. "I imagine so. But don't all principles have their limits? How libertarian, or kind . . . how human can you be, out here?"

"I shouldn't have told you."

"I'm glad you did."

Then, briskly, as if she, too, fled something, the woman said: "The truth is bound to come out when your fleet returns to Earth, so we'll need to work out a defense for you. Or is necessity enough?"

"It doesn't matter." He raised his head, and now he could again speak steadily. "I don't figure to skulk more than I must. Let them say what they will, eight decades from now. I'll already have been judged."

"What?" She retreated a little, perhaps to see the gaunt form better. "You don't mean you'll stay on Rustum? But it isn't necessary!"

"A liar . . . quite likely a murderer . . . I am not worthy to be the master of a ship." His voice cracked over. "And maybe, after all, there isn't going to be anymore space travel to come home to."

He jerked free of her and went through the door. She stared after him. She had better let him out; no, the key had been left in the bulkhead lock. She had no excuse to follow.

You aren't alone, Joshua, she wanted to call. *Every one of us is beside you. Time is the bridge that always burns behind us.*

THE END